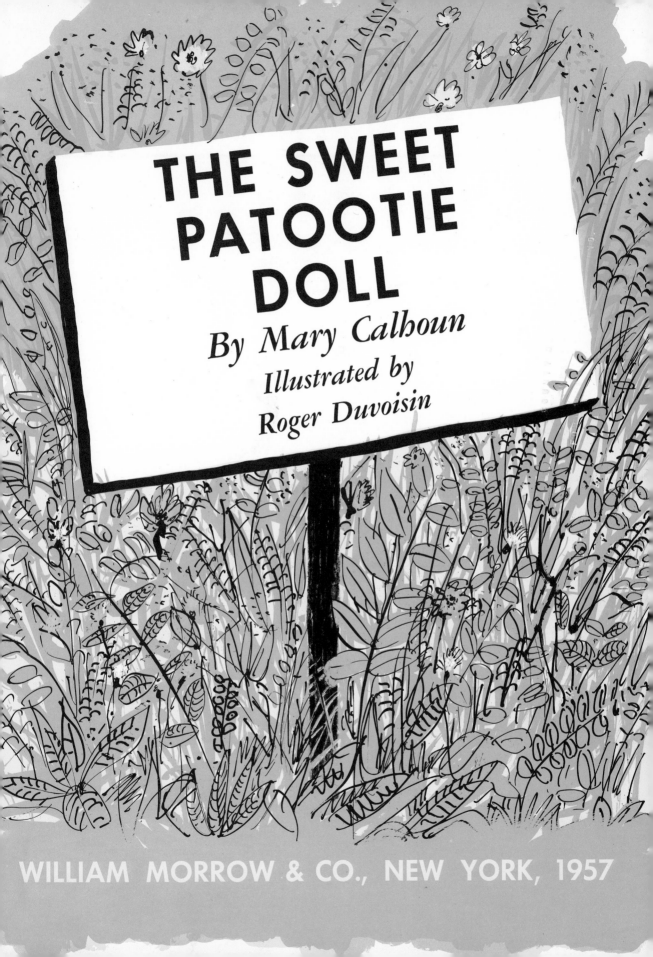

THE SWEET PATOOTIE DOLL

By *Mary Calhoun*

Illustrated by
Roger Duvoisin

WILLIAM MORROW & CO., NEW YORK, 1957

To
MICHAEL and GREGORY
who wanted a story one day

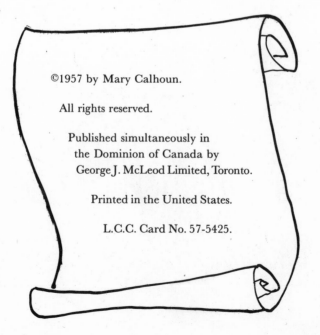

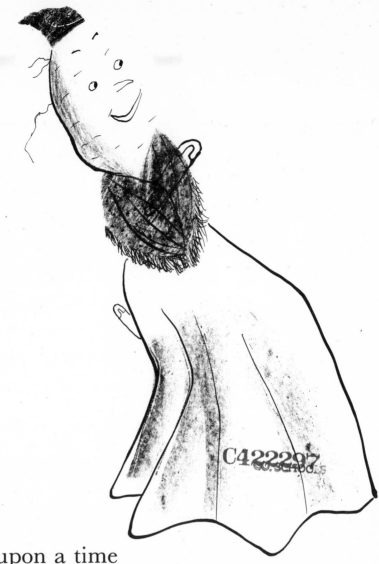

Once upon a time
there was a Sweet Patootie Doll.
What's that? Why, a doll made
out of a sweet potato, of course!
Well, this little old Sweet Patootie Doll
belonged to a girl named Lucy.
And this is how the doll came to be.

Lucy lived on the tiptop of Stony Bald,
with her Mam and her Pap
and old Houn' Dog.
She didn't have a cat.
She didn't even have a doll.
So one end-of-winter day,
Lucy climbed down into the root cellar
and she found an old brown sweet potato.

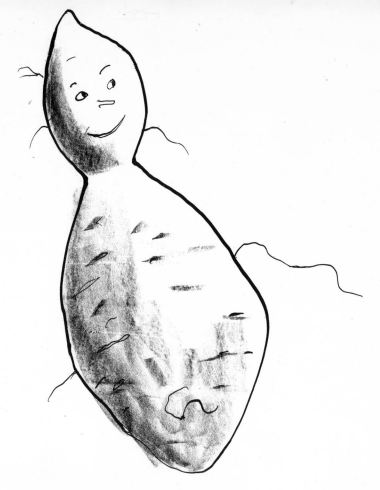

It had a bump on one end,
just right for a head.
And the bump had two specks,
just right for eyes,
and a brown, curvy scratch,
just right for a mouth.
Lucy tied a yellow handkerchief
around the sweet potato for a skirt,
and a piece of blue wool for a shawl.
And for a bonnet?

Why, the cut-off thumb
of Lucy's worn-out mitten, for sure!
Then Lucy loved it and loved it
until it was the Sweet Patootie Doll.

Every day
Lucy and the Sweet Patootie Doll
played together.
On sunny days, with spring coming on,
they had tea parties.
Every sunny afternoon,
a tea party on the old stump
in the side yard.
"Won't you have tea,
Miss Sweet Patootie Doll?"
Lucy would say,
pouring water into an acorn.
And the Sweet Patootie Doll's curvy mouth
would smile a big brown smile.
One afternoon they were playing tea party,
when Lucy's mother called her.
Lucy ran into the house
and forgot the Sweet Patootie Doll.
So the doll just sat on the stump
in the sunshine,
smiling her big brown smile.

Pretty soon, old Mr. Coon
came sniffing along.
When that coon smelled
the Sweet Patootie Doll, he said to himself,
"Aha! Sweet potato for dinner!"

Up to the stump he scampered
and grabbed the doll in his mouth,
and off to the piney woods he ran.
First he headed for the brook,

for he thought he had better wash his paws
before he ate.
He washed as careful as any coon
on Stony Bald mountain.
Then he turned around
to eat the Sweet Patootie Doll.

But the Sweet Patootie Doll
just smiled and smiled.
Because she knew what she was for.
And it wasn't for eating.

When Mr. Coon saw that smile
it made him feel so queer
that he turned tail and ran.
Somehow, he didn't want
sweet potato for dinner, after all.

All by herself,
the Sweet Patootie Doll lay on the grass,
while a mockingbird called sweetly
from a black-haw bush.
Wasn't long, though,

before Silly Young Fox came bouncing along.

He spied the bright bonnet.

Sniff, snuffle!

He smelled the Sweet Patootie Doll.

"Aha!" said he to himself.
"Sweet potato for dinner! Hi ho!"
And he snatched up the Sweet Patootie Doll.
Off he ran

to find a quiet place to eat her.
But the Sweet Patootie Doll
just smiled her big brown smile.
Because she knew what she was for.
And it wasn't for dinner.

Silly Young Fox never did find
that quiet spot, though.
For crash, *clump*, GROWL!
Here came Old Man B'ar,
looking for dinner.
"I smell sweet potato!" he growled.

Silly Young Fox dropped that doll
like a hot potato
and zipped his bushy red tail
away into the woods.
"Grumph, yum!"
Old Man B'ar smacked his lips
as he got his paws
on the Sweet Patootie Doll.
But the Sweet Patootie Doll just smiled.
Because she knew what she was for.

And it wasn't for Old Man B'ar.
Just then "Aroof! Aro-o-of!"
came ringing through the trees.

It was Houn' Dog,
smelling out Old Man B'ar.
Old Man B'ar dropped the doll
and shuffled himself away from those parts,
faster than JUMP!
"Aro-o-of! Snuffle, Snuffle!"

Houn' Dog followed Old Man B'ar's trail.
"Snuffle, Snuff!"—
right up to where Sweet Patootie Doll lay
under a pink dogwood tree.

"Snuff!" said Houn' Dog in surprise.
"A big sweet potato!"
He couldn't see very well,
so he didn't know
that the potato was Lucy's doll.
"I'll just bury this in my bone pile,"
Houn' Dog told himself.

So away went Sweet Patootie Doll
in Houn' Dog's mouth.
But she just smiled
the same as ever before.
Because she knew what she was for.
And it wasn't for burying.

A leap and a bound.
And there they were,
right back in Lucy's side yard.
Just as Houn' Dog came
to the old tree stump,
he heard Pap calling him.

PLUMP! on the stump,
he dropped the Sweet Patootie Doll.

Lucy came skipping out of the house then,
looking for her doll.
She spied her on the stump.

"Why, poor old Sweet Patootie Doll,"
she laughed.
"You've been waiting here for me
all the time.
I'm sorry I forgot you."
She picked up the doll
and hugged her, hard.

And the Sweet Patootie Doll
just smiled her big brown smile.
Because she knew what she was for—
for making a little girl glad.